Splash-a-Roo and Snowflakes

SPLASH-A-ROO AND SNOWFLAKES

BY MICHELLE POPLOFF
ILLUSTRATED BY DIANE PALMISCIANO

A Yearling First Choice Chapter Book

For Mary, Beverly, and Craig—
with thanks and great affection
—M. P.

To N. M.,
who helped me discover the inner picture.
—D. P.

Published by
Bantam Doubleday Dell Publishing Group, Inc.
1540 Broadway
New York, New York 10036
Text copyright © 1996 by Michelle Poploff
Illustrations copyright © 1996 by Diane Palmisciano
All rights reserved.

Library of Congress Cataloging-in-Publication Data

The hardback of this title is cataloged as follows:
Poploff, Michelle.
Splash-a-roo and snowflakes / by Michelle Poploff; illustrated by
Diane Palmisciano.
p.   cm.
"A Yearling First Choice Chapter Book."
Summary: Best friends Emma and Kate turn a boring winter day into
a trip to the beach by using their imaginations.
ISBN 0-385-32176-7 (alk. paper). — ISBN 0-440-41119-X (pbk. : alk. paper)
[1. Beaches—Fiction. 2. Imagination—Fiction. 3. Play—Fiction.]
I. Palmisciano, Diane, ill. II. Title.
PZ7.P7957Sp   1996
[E]—dc20   95-21362   CIP   AC

Hardcover: The trademark Delacorte Press® is registered in the U.S. Patent and
Trademark Office and in other countries.

Paperback: The trademark Yearling® is registered in the U.S. Patent and
Trademark Office and in other countries.

The text of this book is set in 17-point Baskerville.
Manufactured in the United States of America
February 1996
10 9 8 7 6 5 4 3 2 1

CONTENTS

1. TWO GRUMPY GIRLS

Emma and Kate were very best friends.

Sometimes they played at Emma's house.

Other times they stayed at Kate's.

Today they were at Emma's.

It was a cold, gray winter Sunday.

The girls were grumpy.

They could not think of one thing to do.

"What a boring Sunday," Emma said.

Emma looked out her window.

She touched the glass.

Her finger felt wet and cold.

Kate twirled her

purple-polka-dot hair bow.

She wore a purple something every day.

"I wish it was summer right now,"
Kate said.

"So do I," said Emma.

"But summer is a long time away."
Kate raised her hands over her head.
She pretended to dive into water.
"Splash," she said.

"I wish we were in the ocean."

Emma faced her friend.

She snapped her fingers.

"That's a great idea," she said.

"What is?" asked Kate.

She was twirling her purple bow again.

"Let's pretend it's summer," Emma said.

"We can go to the beach."

Kate folded her arms across her chest.

"No way, Emma," she said.

Kate pointed to Emma's window.

"It's freezing outside."

Emma flipped on the light switch.

The room felt warm and cozy.

"Who cares," she said.

"We'll have a Sun Day inside."

Kate shook her head.

The purple bow jiggled back and forth.

"You and your big ideas," she said.

"Give it a try," Emma said.

"It will be fun.

We'll put swimsuits on over our clothes."

"My suits are packed away at home,"
Kate said.

"No big deal," said Emma.

"You can wear one of mine."

"Can I wear your sunglasses?"
Kate asked.

"Sure," Emma said.

"I have two pairs.

And I'll get my straw hat."

Finally Kate grinned.

She grabbed Emma's arm.

The girls swung around in a circle.

"Our own winter beach party,"
Kate said.

"What are we waiting for?"

2. FUN IN THE SUN

Emma found two swimsuits
in her bottom drawer.
"Look, this has purple flowers,"
Emma said.
She tossed it to Kate.

Then Emma pulled on a rainbow suit
over her clothes.

Kate looked at the swimsuit she wore.

"It doesn't match my bow."

"I'll fix that," Emma said.

"Now you see it."

She stuck her straw hat on Kate's head.

"Now you don't."

"No fair, Emma," Kate said.

Emma handed Kate pink sunglasses.

"Pink begins with
the same letter as purple.
That's close enough," Emma said.

"You're so bossy, Emma," said Kate.

"You're so stuck on purple," Emma said.

She reached for her sunglasses.

They were red with silver sparkles.

She pulled Kate over to the mirror.

"Ta da," said Emma.

"Is that us?" Kate asked.

Emma grinned.

"Now what do you think?" she asked.

Slowly Kate smiled.

"I think I like it," she said.

"What's next?"

Emma pushed her sunglasses
down her nose.

"Follow me," she said.

Emma opened the hall closet.

"Dig in," she said to Kate.

Emma found a blue beach blanket.

Kate found a flat beach ball.

"Here's sunscreen lotion," Emma said.

"Smell this."

She held it under Kate's nose.

"Just like the beach," Kate said.

"There's even sand stuck to the cap."

Then she rubbed lotion
on both their noses.

"Help me move this thing," Emma said.

"It weighs a ton."

They tugged a red beach umbrella

into Emma's room.

Kate spread the beach blanket.

Emma looked around her room.

She saw her shells on her bookcase.

"Now we'll really feel like
we're on the beach," she said.
Emma put the shells around the blanket.
"Don't forget snacks," Kate said.
"How about juice and crackers?"
Emma asked.
"That sounds good," Kate said.
"Be right back," said Emma.

Kate blew up the beach ball.

Emma was back soon.

They hit the ball back
and forth twenty times.

"That's the best we've ever done,"
said Emma.

"I'm hungry," said Kate. "And thirsty."

"Same for me," said Emma.

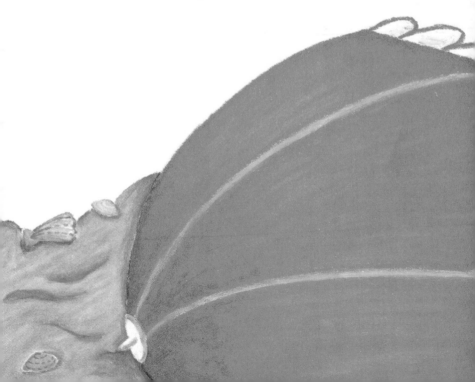

The girls sat under the beach umbrella.

Emma tickled Kate's toes.

"You have big feet," Emma said.

She put her foot next to Kate's.

"Yours are smaller," Kate said.

"But they stink."

She pinched her nose shut.

"Let's eat."

They drank juice and ate crackers.

"This is fun," Emma said.

"We're all alone at the beach."

"No rude boys to bug us," said Kate.

"Watch this," Emma said.

She dipped a cracker into her cup.

"Yum. Try my secret salty drink,"
she said.

Kate leaned over.

Some juice spilled on her arm.

"Watch out. You're splashing me,"
Kate said.

She splashed some of her juice on Emma.

"Splash-a-roo to you," said Emma.

"Let's call this drink our Sun Day
Splash-a-Roo."

"You were right, Emma," Kate said.

"We turned our Sunday
into a real Sun Day."

"I knew we could do it," said Emma.

"Still, I wish —"

"What's going on in here?"
a boy's voice asked.

3. BUG BROTHER

Emma and Kate sat up quickly.

They bumped heads.

Their sunglasses clunked together.

Kate's straw hat fell off.

Emma's brother, Josh,

poked his head through the doorway.

"We're having a winter beach party,"
Emma said. "It's private.
No boys allowed."
"Every beach needs a lifeguard," Josh said.
He stuck one foot into the room.
"I'm your man."
Kate giggled.
"I don't mind," she whispered to Emma.
"You'll be sorry," Emma whispered back.
"Quit whispering," said Josh.
"All right, you can stay," Emma said.
"But you're not a lifeguard.
You're an ugly beach bug."

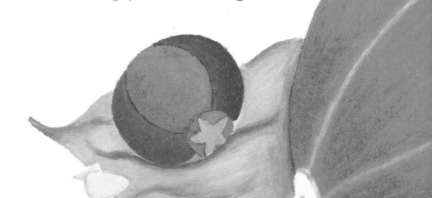

"Bugga, bugga, bugga," said Josh.

He flopped down on the floor.

He moved in a creepy-crawly way.

"Bugga boo," Josh yelled.

He fell on Kate.

Kate grabbed Emma.

Josh grabbed a handful of crackers.
"I'm one hungry beach bug,"
he squeaked.
"Too bad you don't have any sandwiches.
Get it? Sand-wiches."

Josh stuck out his legs.

"Watch out for my shells," Emma said.

Kate leaned closer to Emma.

"How do we get rid of a beach bug?"
she whispered.

"Wait for my signal," Emma said.

"This won't take long."

"What were you wishing for anyway?"
Josh asked.
Bits of cracker fell out of his mouth.
"I was wishing for real sand," said Emma.
"We could build a sand castle," said Kate.
"Or bury a beach bug," Emma said.
She rubbed her hands together.
"Let's squash this big bug!"
Emma shouted. "Now!"

4. SNOWFLAKE SURPRISE

The girls jumped on Josh.

They tickled his feet and ribs.

Josh finally rolled away.

He jumped up.

Emma and Kate fell back on the rug.

Josh looked out Emma's window.

"We can build something better

than a sand castle," Josh said.

He pointed to the window.

The girls looked out.

"It's snowing!" Emma and Kate shouted.

They hugged each other.

"Let's go outside," Emma said.

She reached for her socks.

"We'll build a snowman."

"I didn't bring boots," Kate said.

"Here we go again," Emma said.

"I have an extra pair."

"I just hope...," Kate said.

"Sorry. No purple boots," Emma said.

"I know that, silly," Kate said.

"I just hope your boots fit.

Remember, I have big feet."

Emma laughed. "Not that big.

Put your socks on.

My boots are downstairs."

Kate looked around the room.

"What about our beach party?" she said.

"It will still be here," Emma said.

She looked at Josh.

"Besides, that beach bug
ate up all the food."

"We can have hot cocoa later," Kate said.

Emma turned off the light.

"Not so fast," Josh said.

"You forgot something."

Kate and Emma looked at each other.

"What?" they asked.

Josh laughed.

"Your swimsuits and sunglasses," he said.

"See you outside."

Emma looked down.

"I almost forgot," she said.

"Let's keep the suits and sunglasses on."

She tapped her sparkly red pair.

"These can be our snowglasses.

No one else will have them."

Kate nodded.

"And no one else has summer
and winter in one day."

"Let's go before the snow stops,"
Emma said.
Kate put the straw hat
on the beach blanket.
The purple-polka-dot bow
fell out of her hair.

"Let's build a snowgirl.

We can put the bow on her head,"

Kate said.

"She can wear my sunglasses,"

said Emma.

She shut her bedroom door.

"I'll race you down," she said.

"Last one out loves beach bugs."

Michelle Poploff is the author of the Busy O'Brien books, including *Busy O'Brien and the Great Bubble Blowout* and *Busy O'Brien and the Caterpillar Punch Bunch*. She lives in New York City.

Diane Palmisciano is the author and illustrator of *Garden Partners* and has illustrated many more books, including *Second Grade Friends* and *Second Grade Friends Again* by Miriam Cohen. She lives in Cambridge, Massachusetts.